# About the

*Photo credit: Kay Hickman*

CB Fletcher has been writing stories since she could spell and scribble letters. She has a passion for stories that journey to self-discovery or great epic tales, and anything in-between. CB has been published in two collaborative books and several digital and print publications in the United States. Her writing has always been heavily supported by her family, who are avid readers and enjoy unique art. The main character of this story is named after her mother, who inspired the tale when she requested a story about watermelon for her birthday...

"No matter how it looks, have faith in the seed that is planted within you to grow your unique prosperity." — CB Fletcher.

# QUEEN CLARICE AND THE WATERMELON SEED

# C B FLETCHER

---

## QUEEN CLARICE
## AND THE
## WATERMELON SEED

Nightingale Books

A CIP catalogue record for this title is
available from the British Library.
ISBN 978 83875 336 8

*Nightingale Books is an imprint of*
*Pegasus Elliot MacKenzie Publishers Ltd.*
www.pegasuspublishers.com

First Published in 2022

**Nightingale Books**
**Sheraton House Castle Park**
**Cambridge England**

Printed & Bound in Great Britain

# Dedication

For my mother, Susan Claire Westbrook Fletcher, who
planted the seeds in me to create my oasis.

# Acknowledgments

Thank you to my family, blood, and otherwise, that have walked with me through my desert as I sought to create a unique life of my own. Thank you for giving me a reason to keep going even when it got rough, Marcus, Jalen, Amelia, and Zuri.

# One

A rare cloud passed over the barren desert giving shade to a red ant colony on the spring crescent celebration day for Queen Rae. While the colony loved and respected their queen, her reign was filled with the love of tradition and empty stomachs. Unless scraps from campers and passersby dropped down or water was brought from a cactus.

\*\*\*

Five generations ago, Red Ants, Bees, Scorpions, and Sphinx moths all lived in an oasis. The different colonies were surrounded by fruitful bushes, lush grass, and tall slender trees. The Red Ant colony was built out of red clay and gold carving with wooden doors to royal chambers. Cheerful songs and joyful voices ran through the thriving community for all who lived there. The Bees provided honey and maintained plant life. The peaceful Sphinx moths watched over the land with graceful protection and assisted the Bees; both clans lived in the trees surrounding the oasis. The

Scorpions protected the ants as they worked on irrigation channels and carried seeds to be planted and they lived in rock formations that surrounded the oasis. They coexisted peacefully with the humans surrounding the oasis that enjoyed the space as part of a resort.

The oasis colony tracked their ages by the cycle of the waning crescent moon, which signified new beginnings and creation. Most in the colonies and clans would live to be sixty crescents. Which allowed kings and queens to have children for many years before passing on their crowns. However, the first Red Ant Queen Carrie did not allow herself to have a king because she thought it would be a distraction, which became the tradition.

Five generations later on the first spring crescent, Princess Rae of the Red Ant Colony, Prince Cylon of the Scorpion clan, Princess Ayo of the Bee clan, and Prince Larry of the Sphinx Moth clan celebrated their birthdays under the moonlight with a great spring harvest feast. Over many moons, Princess Rae would lead them into fun mischievous acts that Cylon would support, Ayo would be nervous about, and Larry would scuttle along, anxiously, in his caterpillar form. Princess Rae would bring along her assigned best friend, Croz, to be the lookout and they'd spy on humans to see what new food they could get then return with their treasures and hide in Princess Rae's honey gold-adorned room to enjoy the food.

On the eighth crescent celebration, the oasis was pillaged by Princess Mala and her Bush Spider clan. The violent attack frightened the humans away that were vacationing on the land. The Sphinx moths and Bees fled while the scorpions and ants remained to the devastation of the friends. As time went on, the weeping about the attack and separation of the colonies faded into dust just as the oasis did. Fortunately, the alliance with the scorpions continued per tradition and they protected the ant colony. The longtime friends shared food when they could, scarce as it was.

One day, the princess became Queen Rae and ruled with love and discipline but had great concern for her starving colony; however, her commitment to tradition overruled her fears for her loyal ants. Upon her ascension, she named her friend Croz to be the general. Starting from her twenty-third crescent, she had forty daughters that she gave numbers instead of names, based on their strength and personalities. She loved her daughters, but only a select few were groomed to be queen, and the others were to serve her as queen's ladies. The successor would be given a name. Like the ladies-in-waiting, the queen's soldiers and guards were nameless unless they held a leadership position such as a lieutenant or general, in which the queen would name them to be distinguishable among the soldiers.

***

The queen had lived through thirty-eight crescent moons, and while her antennas were still perked, they would droop down, and this was the sign for an aging queen to pass on her knowledge and support for the next queen. As the sun began to set and the moon peeked through the single cloud, the grand colony bustled with ants scurrying from the smallest tunnel to the highest chamber that surrounded the tall underground cavern. From the queen's ladies to the workers, rumors spread of another girl being born, and more ridiculous rumors spread that General Croz would marry the queen. Another spread that the queen was stepping down. Lady One was informed of the truth and spread it to all the queen's ladies.

Everyone began to gather under the queen's chamber entrance. The elegant entrance, formed into a podium, was made through generations of melted beeswax and honeycomb, giving off a radiant golden glow and fading sweet smell. The queen's ladies stood in front of the stirring crowd and prepared to celebrate the news that they'd gained a new sister. They had dried flowers in their hands to toss and their royal orange and yellow silk scarves around their necks. Lady One held an ornate yellow blanket she had sewn together as she had for other queens' ladies. Lady Two inched her way to the front and whispered to Lady One, "You're happy about having another sister?"

"Of course I am," Lady One replied with a grin.

"But that means more competition to be selected by the queen," Lady Two explained.

"Oh dear, sister, you forget that I am Lady One. I have been Lady One for fifteen crescents and have been groomed to be queen more than any of you. I see this new sister as another one of my loyal ladies, not a threat. Now smile and welcome our sister," Lady One said with an evil grin.

The queen gracefully glided out of her chambers in her purple cotton robe, woven together with silk and golden crown, with two soldiers at her sides as celebratory drums were played and the crowd roared. General Croz followed behind her holding the new baby in perfectly softened cotton. Queen Rae smiled and waved at the adoring crowd then lowered her hands to silence them.

"Colony, I come before you today joyful! On this day of the 38th crescent moon, I have the honor to introduce to you, my new daughter!" Queen Rae announced, and the crowd cheered. She eased the crowd by lowering her hands and continuing, "And to finally name the lady who will be my successor."

Everyone quivered in anxious joy and cheered. The excitement shook the colony walls. The queen's ladies jumped up and down. Lady Two gleefully tore off her scarf and tied it to Lady One's other scarves to make her appear more elegant then pushed Lady One toward the steps to walk up and take her place as queen. Just as she began to strut toward the towering golden balcony, Queen Rae bellowed, "Ladies and Gentleants, I present to you, Princess Clarice!"

She snatched the baby from General Croz and held her up for the crowd to see. The colony jumped up and cheered as celebratory drums and horns echoed from chamber to chamber inspiring all to dance. Many of the queen's ladies' mouths dropped in shock, then they shrugged and joined in the colony's celebratory dance by waving their scarves above their heads mimicking a whirling wind and belting a melodious tune. Princess Clarice peeked up from the blanket and smiled and waved at her new loyal ants. General Croz took the new princess into his arms as she smiled at her mother who clapped in celebration. Princess Clarice was lowered as a soldier walked over with a red blanket and small gold woven crown decorated with a single ruby jewel. Queen Rae grabbed the crown, placed it on Clarice's head, grabbed the blanket, wrapped her in it, and held her above the cheering crowd again. Lady One stood frozen in disappointment and shook in anger. Lady Two patted her back and calmly said, "She is still our sister and will one day be our queen. We must respect our queen's decision. I know you're disappointed, but you can still go to our mother and talk to her about her decision and maybe she will explain why she chose the baby. She does love us all. It will be okay."

"Yeah, but she loved me the most. You all were raised to serve; I was created to lead. How could she do this? She is an old mindless queen that has made a mistake. I will show her how great I am and how wrong she is. Wait and see," Lady One stated angrily and threw the blanket down as she stomped off.

Over the next eighteen crescent moon cycles, Princess Clarice was loved by the colony and taught all the ways of a queen by her mother and sisters, except Lady One. She focused on how to replace Clarice for many crescents. She and Lady Two would find ways to torment their little sister to make her question her confidence. They stole and hid her royal scarves and told the queen that the princess had thrown them away. They would try to ruin her crescent celebrations by tripping her and snatching her royal jewel and making her fetch it. Sometimes they'd spread rumors about how the queen was changing her mind about Clarice. No matter what they did Clarice would lift her head and walk with pride.

Unfortunately, the conditions of the colony worsened and worried Queen Rae. Soldiers journeyed to search for food but often brought back dried half-eaten scraps that would barely feed the colony. The red clay walls dried out more and more. The ornate entrance, with ancient carvings filled with gold, glistened less and less. The wooden doorways to the queen's ladies and General Croz's suites began to brittle, except for the queen's door, which remained decorated in gold and wood. Princess Clarice resided in her private chamber with layers of purple silk curtains that quieted her space from the bustling colony. Her sister, Lady Seven, four crescents older, would sneak through the curtains with pieces of dried berries from the royal stash to tell her stories so she wouldn't be afraid.

Queen Rae thought about abandoning their home, but her commitment to tradition outweighed her courage to leave.

# Two

One sizzling afternoon, Princess Clarice awakened in her silky bed made from tumbleweed, cotton, and the hundreds of scarves from past queen's ladies. Her arm laid above her head and rested atop the royal piece of ruby in her crown. She flicked the ruby around as she stared at her ceiling made of old honeycomb and thought back to a moment when her mother reminded her of her birthright.

After her fifth crescent celebration, she and her mother sat cradled on the floor of her room covered in her sisters' scattered, celebratory scarves and gifts. Queen Rae gently explained.

"Since our beginning, the room's walls of young royals were covered in honeycomb."

"Why, Mama? It's sticky," Princess Clarice asked.

"Because honey symbolizes abundance and the honeycomb, our colony, must work to keep our abundance. Our allies, the bees, taught us this. They told Carrie, our first queen, that when the honey is gone, we must find a way to put it back in the honeycomb so that there is hope for the future. So, as a princess, you must carry this burden to make sure we survive. You sleep in a honeycomb room to remind you of this," Queen Rae explained.

"But we're ants. Not bees. It's not our job to make the honey. It's our job to build the colony and make our way to survive," Princess Clarice said.

Queen Rae sighed and laughed. "Oh, my young girl, exactly."

Princess Clarice sighed as she remembered her burden then sat up from her bed, stretched, and rubbed her eyes. Lady Seven, five crescents older, approached the chamber with fresh water in a small bowl. She curtsied and slowly shuffled into the room, as her light blue scarf gently glided behind her.

"How did you sleep, your highness?" Lady Seven asked.

"Like an ant with a colony on her shoulders," Clarice said grieved by her responsibility.

Lady Seven chuckled. "Sounds heavy."

Lady Seven walked over to Clarice and held the bowl so that she could begin to wash her face.

Clarice cupped the water in her hands, splashed it all over her face quickly, and said, "Lady Seven."

"Yes, Miss?" Lady Seven answered timidly.

"Do you know why I sleep in the honeycomb room?" Clarice asked as she finished and shook the water from her hands.

"Yes, Your Highness," Lady Seven answered as she placed the bowl down and handed her sister a small cotton ball to dry her face.

"What do you and your chamber sisters sleep under? I've never been down there in all these crescents," Clarice asked.

"We sleep under you, Sis — Your Highness, but we can smell the honeycomb," Lady Seven stated, knowing the burden that her sister holds in her heart. She smirked and gently put her hand on Clarice's shoulder and said, "Should I prepare breakfast for you, Your Highness? The scavenger team was able to find some cactus today."

Princess Clarice held her sister's hand and laid her head on it affectionately. Then gently pushed her away.

"Share whatever they have found with my sisters; we have a colony to run. I am on my own today, going out. Not a word to our mother... *Or you're banished*," Clarice commanded and joked.

Lady Seven chuckled and shook her head as the princess scurried out of her golden room and crept along the rigid, flaking, red clay wall down to the soldiers' chamber. When she entered the chamber and crept towards the armory, a lieutenant and soldier passed by, and she grabbed his quartz side dagger from his weapon pouch. The lieutenant swiftly turned around nearly drawing his sword and she playfully grinned. He put his sword away and the other soldier chuckled.

"You should mind how you sneak up on a soldier, Princess," the lieutenant scolded and smirked.

"And a soldier should mind his surroundings so he can't be snuck up on... Cactus," Clarice said with a smile as he rolled his eyes and grinned.

"I wish you'd stop calling me that," Cactus stated.

The soldier was puzzled and asked, "Lieutenant Anthony, why does she call you Cactus?"

"No reason," Cactus said as he playfully rolled his eyes, then smirked and continued, "What can we do for you, Princess?" Cactus asked and smiled.

"Need some armor and your small blade. I'm going out today," Princess Clarice stated.

"Under what order? There's not another scavenging run or perimeter observance today. A Princess never leaves without escort or purpose unless it is a matter of war," Cactus said sternly.

The soldier chortled and nudged Cactus then said, "What's she going to fight out there a pebble?"

Cactus snapped his head and glared at the soldier until he cowered to the disciplinary look as Princess Clarice rolled her eyes and huffed at her friend and lieutenant.

"I just want to go out and check on a few things. It's a lovely day," Clarice coyly replied.

"Your Highness, again, a royal does not leave the colony without a proper escort or reason. Under the order of the queen, I cannot allow you to take the armor and leave the colony unattended," Cactus explained gently and firmly.

"Well, if you're so protective why don't you follow me out there?" Princess Clarice suggested.

Cactus became annoyed and said, "You clearly want me to lose my job."

Against their better judgment, the soldiers searched for some spare armor so she wouldn't be recognized. They brought back some rusted armor that had been tarnished with the markings of battles over generations. She took a deep breath to ready herself for their excursion, then smiled and put on the chest plate and arm protection. Cactus removed her royal stone and tied it around her neck gently. The friends smirked at each other, and Cactus nodded his head insisting that they get going on their mischievous adventure.

The three of them crept up to the entrance of the colony, dodging ants bustling out of their living quarters to get to their task for the day. The Princess kept her head turned to the side and ducked behind Lieutenant Cactus' shoulder so she wouldn't be recognized. Ants carrying cotton to the queen's bed chambers nearly knocked over the princess.

Another group of mothers chased after their children towards their school and a little girl recognized Princess Clarice. They winked at each other, and both went on their way. When the trio made it to the top, Princess Clarice hugged Cactus to thank him, and the accompanying soldier's mouth dropped. Cactus quickly released from the embrace and they both went back into their proper stances with their backs straightened and heads held high.

"Okay, you two watch my back," Princess Clarice instructed.

"We should go with you, Highness," Cactus said.

"No. One of you stay in here and another at the top where you can see me. Just alert me of any disturbances," Princess Clarice demanded.

"What should we look out for?" the other soldier said.

"Bush spiders. And more terrifying, my mother," Princess Clarice explained.

"Yes, Your Highness." The soldiers laughed.

Princess Clarice smirked and ran out of the entrance. She saw a truck that was four hundred steps away and started jogging towards the truck, but the intense heat wore her down to a slow dragging walk. She turned and saw that Cactus was concerned and about to run to her, so she waved to him and gave a thumbs-up to signal that she was all right. Then she balled up her fist to signal that she was stopping and resting and collapsed onto the ground to take a breath. Cactus shook his head and started to walk toward her.

Suddenly, there was a strong breeze and a big shadow above her that woke her up. When she looked up, she saw an object falling toward her and was mesmerized. It was so odd, red, and huge.

SPLAT!

Princess Clarice's head was stuck tilted to the side from her joyful curiosity as the piece of fruit now surrounded her body.

"This… Is not good," Princess Clarice thought while she lay stuck in the fruit.

Cactus saw the fruit fall on her and immediately panicked and yelled, "Soldier, gather the royal guards now! Princess Clarice is hurt!"

His call echoed throughout the colony and sent everyone into a frenzy. Soldiers, colony members, and Queen's ladies scurried around trying to get more information and get help to her. Even some rumors spread saying that she was kidnapped and worse, killed.

Meanwhile, Clarice lay in the fruit and tried to breathe. When she did, she sucked in some of the fruit's juices and started to nibble around her. She took another bite and another, and more while she enjoyed the sweet fruit and wriggled herself free. When she got to the top of the fruit, she saw the soldiers and half of the colony rushing out to her aid and to spectate; with Cactus leading the pack.

"Princess! Are you all right? Don't worry more soldiers are coming!" Cactus yelled as he ran up to the fruit.

"I'm fine, I'm fine. Look at this food! Call for the Queen," Clarice ordered excitedly.

Ants came out in dozens and gathered around as they excitedly touched the fruit. Princess Clarice walked on all sides of the fruit and picked off small pieces then tossed them to the giggling children. As the humans sat and ate, they were unaware of the large crowd of ants that had formed under the truck. She stood up and bellowed, "It's good, isn't it? I think a lot of fruit like this could help with our food shortage! This is so wonderful and sweet! It's water and food all in one! We must bring more back to the colony!"

They cheered and agreed. She spoke proudly about her journey out of the colony and how she discovered the fruit. Cactus looked up to her proud of her recovery but sunk his head because he thought he failed to protect her. Just as she was talking about her escape, General Croz stood at the top of the anthill and bellowed, "THE QUEEN APPROACHES!"

Armed soldiers quickly marched out of the colony, followed by the queen's ladies wearing bright blue, orange, red, and yellow royal scarves.

The soldiers formed in lines and shapes as the queen's ladies danced and twirled through them. Next, a lieutenant blew a horn and signaled four other soldiers to play the drums. The queen's ladies snatched off their scarves and waved them as they shook their hips and heads. They shimmied toward the crowd as the soldiers split them apart and created a path for the ladies. The dancing ladies tied their scarves together and lifted them in the air, creating colorful shadows on the ground. They all lowered their scarves in unison and revealed Queen Rae standing on top of the colony in her gold woven crown with quartz crystals and a royal purple scarf. As she walked, the ladies raised their scarves above her head, and she gracefully nodded at her subjects while she passed under.

When she reached the fruit, General Croz gracefully assisted her up to the top to join the princess. The queen raised her eyebrow and pursed her lips at Princess Clarice, while she picked the pieces of fruit stuck on her daughter's body. Princess Clarice swatted away her mother's arm, sighed annoyingly, and said, "Mom, I know we don't leave the colony unless we meet with the scorpions, but is this performance necessary every time we do leave? No one else is here to see it but the same ants in the colony!"

"When you are Queen, my daughter, you may leave or enter the colony however you like during important matters. But until then, be careful what you say. I am still Queen and I know what I like. And it's *Your Majesty*," Queen Rae whispered sternly.

"Yes, Your Majesty," Princess Clarice whispered as she lowered her eyes and stepped back.

Queen Rae raised her head proudly, turned to the colony, and announced, "My good ants, I understand that you all have questions about what Princess Clarice has discovered. But I tell you not to fear it. It is just a piece of fruit."

"But Princess Clarice said that there was water in this and food. It could save our colony from starvation. It is what we need, Your Majesty," a brave citizen cried out.

Queen Rae slowly turned around and gave a stern look to her daughter. Princess Clarice stood firmly on the watermelon with a straight face and firm eyes to hide her deep quivering breaths. Queen Rae slowly approached the princess and scolded her.

"What did you tell these poor little ants? They are starving! Not to mention gullible beyond measure. How are you going to provide this for everyone? I do not want to give false hope to my colony."

"Our colony, Mother-Majesty! I came out here to see what our options were, besides drying cactus and sand. Don't think that you are the only one who cares about the well-being of this colony. This landed on me, and it is nutritious and filling. If we can find more, we can survive," Princess Clarice explained passionately.

Queen Rae rolled her eyes and snidely smirked, "My silly ambitious daughter. Don't you see this came from humans? It fell on you, silly little ant. If this is how you are going to operate, then you are not fit to rule my colony."

She turned her back to Clarice and explained to her ants that this food source would be examined and not to touch it until further notice. Princess Clarice annoyingly sighed at her mother's proclamation.

As the Queen was helped down from the watermelon, Clarice shouted out an idea, "Ants! I am asking for your attention and cooperation."

Queen Rae snapped her head at Clarice and loudly whispered, "What do you think you're doing?"

Princess Clarice ignored her and continued to speak. "My good ants, I am asking you to trust me and continue to explore this fruit. I know it is strange and large and from the humans. But if you are tired of eating small rations of garbage, instead of fruit that is plentiful and sweet, then don't join me on this journey."

Clarice turned and looked down at her mother with a crass look. The queen rolled her eyes and harshly whispered, "If you want to endanger these ants and seek food that we don't even know exists elsewhere, so be it. But it will be the end of my reign and the death of the colony."

Clarice smirked at the queen and said, "I'm willing to risk the end of your reign, for the survival of the colony."

# Three

As the humans made their fire and started their party for the night, Princess Clarice and General Croz paced the dim-lit muggy war room discussing their attack. Cactus stood in a dark corner to listen in on them, with an equal amount of pride and worry for his dear friend. Princess Clarice wore her red and gold cape, woven from dried roses and chamomile flowers. It draped behind her, obnoxiously so, because it was made to comfort a young royal when anxious when a royal planned for war and related matters. It only annoyed the princess who found that it got in the way while she planned, and the smell drove her crazy.

"Only twenty of us should go up there. That jeep should be easy to access," General Croz said. "It's risky but I am proud to serve under you as I have Her Majesty.

"Thank you. The fewer soldiers at risk the better. We will have to make this quick and efficient," Princess Clarice said.

"The scorpions will assist us in securing the perimeter. Do we know where the fruit is?" General Croz said.

"I sent two of my soldiers to scout the location; it is hidden inside a container in the jeep," Lieutenant Cactus interjected as he emerged from the corner.

Princess Clarice smirked at Cactus and continued speaking to General Croz.

"What kind of fruit is it anyway? Mother is furious with me and refuses to tell me more," said Princess Clarice

"It's watermelon. Your mother and I enjoyed it when your grandmother ruled, and we'd sneak off with our friends to grab food from humans. It was a wonderful time," General Croz stated solemnly then continued. "As you know, this colony sat on an oasis plentiful in fruits and flowers and when the humans, moth, and bee clans escaped, our oasis died. Any ideas to seek other food sources have been shut down under colony law — that we are to maintain this colony — which meant never leaving. And we've been struggling ever since. I mean no disrespect, Your Highness."

"That's okay. I am glad that you were willing to tell me what this is. She keeps so much from me but expects me to lead. You are our general and so much more to me," Princess Clarice said as she rubbed Croz's shoulder, then took a deep breath and continued, "Let us hope that this can save our colony, and maybe we can finally move on," Princess Clarice calmly stated.

The two leaders reviewed several different strategies extremely late into the night. Meanwhile, Cactus brought them water and small food scraps then moved back into the corner to watch them work with a prideful smile. They finally created a solid plan that would get them in and out of the human campsite safely. Just before General Croz finished drawing out the final plan, Lady Seventeen and Thirty-nine knocked in the doorway.

"Good evening, Your Highness, General, and Lieutenant. May we have permission to deliver a message from Her Majesty?" Lady Seventeen asked.

Princess Clarice stood tall and said, "Permission granted."

"The queen would like a word with you about the fruit mission," Lady Seventeen stated.

"She has grown impatient and demands to see the plans now," Lady Thirty-nine stated.

Princess Clarice shook her head and said, "It's bad enough to have my mother disapprove of my ideas. But to send her servants, to deliver her words has sunken to a new low. That will be all, ladies. Please return to your chambers and rest well."

The ladies curtsied and scurried back to their chambers. General Croz walked over, put his arm around her, and said, "Your mother is an ant of tradition. Nothing has ever changed and, likely, it never will under her reign. Your Highness, show her the plans, and maybe once she sees them, she will approve, and our colony will be saved. My princess, you are our next queen, so lead like one."

Cactus calmly walked from his corner and stuttered, "Ricey-Princess-Your Highness, I'll be by your side, but if it gets rough out there, I'm taking you and we're leaving. Ordered or not."

Princess Clarice nodded, grabbed the plans, and then stormed through the colony to Queen Rae's grand royal chamber. Her heavy steps almost shook the colony walls as her cape created a rush of wind behind her. As she approached the halls to the queen's chambers, she covered the guard's mouth and ordered him not to announce her. She got to the door and was blocked by Lady One and Lady Two.

"Move out of the way!" Princess Clarice demanded.

"You must let us announce you, baby sister." Lady Two said.

"Her Majesty does not like to be disturbed, unannounced little girl," Lady One said harshly.

"Ladies, she is my mother too. You will address me as *Your Highness* and obey my commands," Princess Clarice said in a stern tone as she stared at Lady One.

"We are under orders not to obey you under any circumstances," Lady Two lied.

"That order comes from Her Majesty herself, Clarice," Lady One lied with an evil smirk.

"How dare you address me without my title!" Princess Clarice shouted and then calmly smirked. "Upon my ascension to Queen, both of you will be relieved of your duties and *maybe* I will let you stay in *my* colony."

"If the queen finds you to be unfit, *I* am next in line to take her place. I was her first choice. Fifteen crescents I waited for my chance, and you just got in the way. When you fail, and you will, I will hire you to weave my new cape," Lady One cruelly stated.

"You will just be *Lady One*: worthless and without a birthright. You have your knowledge and crescents above me, but your soul is more barren than the desert surrounding us. And even as a baby, our mother could see that I am far more qualified than you after the fifteen crescents you have served under her. So, she named me for that sanctified place. But don't worry, I'm generous, my sister. You can try on my capes and continue to dream," Princess Clarice nastily stated, then pushed past the ladies and through the oak door.

# Four

Princess Clarice burst into Queen Rae's ornate chamber and marched toward the bedroom. The chamber was covered in purple silk with a red and gold trim collected from generations of queens, tucked into corners behind an old honeycomb on the ceiling. The plush cotton was tucked tightly into a woven tumbleweed bed with a green and gold silk cover.

Princess Clarice briefly thought about a time when she played hide and seek with her mother and General Croz around and under the bed when she was a baby. She found her mother's sword and pulled it out to playfully swing it at her. Queen Rae and General Croz jumped back in playful fear then took the sword away.

"You're my little warrior, aren't you? One day, I'll show you how to use it properly," said Queen Rae and smiled.

"My little princess shouldn't have to be a warrior just yet." General Croz added with a grin. Queen Rae cut her eyes at him, shook her head, and mouthed *'remember your place.'* He bowed his head and winked at Princess Clarice as he backed away. She continued to smile at him, ignoring her mother's command.

As she inched further into the room, she took deep breaths to chase away her sweet memory and build her strength to speak. Queen Rae emerged from a separate small chamber where she held private meetings wrapped in her gold and purple night robe.

"How dare you walk into this chamber unannounced!" Queen Rae yelled.

"A simple good evening would have suited just fine, Your Majesty," Princess Clarice said sarcastically.

Queen Rae turned her nose up and said, "Do you have any plans to show me?"

Princess Clarice threw the rolled plans onto the floor and folded her arms. The Queen picked them up and looked them over with disapproving eyes. She kept glancing at Clarice with a raised eyebrow as she reviewed the plans to watch her reaction.

"These plans look good. But can you explain them, my princess?" Queen Rae said.

"You have never called me that," Clarice said surprised.

"Can you explain these plans, my princess?" the queen said with a smirk.

Princess Clarice explained that she, the general, and twenty soldiers will climb out of the colony and eighteen will form a line. Clarice and two soldiers will sneak around the side to search for the watermelon. When they find it, they will throw it down and start passing it down the line into the colony. The citizens will collect the food and put it in the central area of the colony. When the last piece is passed, the soldiers will retreat to the colony, and Clarice and the two soldiers will retreat from the side.

"Hmm. And what about your cover?" the queen asked.

"We are relying on our alliance with King Cylon and his scorpions to secure the perimeter and warn us of any bush spider attacks or human disturbance," Princess Clarice answered confidently.

"I see. I know you think I hate you and that I think you are hopeless. I must admit that I have disliked some of your actions, proclamations, and orders. But I've been hard on you to make you a stronger queen. The day you were born I saw a light in your eyes that only a future queen would have. I tried to go by our traditions to choose one of my ladies, but not one of them had the same light that you did. So, I made an executive decision and named you, our princess. I love all your sisters, but you are my most precious," Queen Rae said with a smirk.

"And Lady One? Is she really meant to take my place if I do not serve this colony well?" Princess Clarice asked.

Queen Rae chuckled, cupped Clarice's face, and said, "Lady One is only meant to be Lady One. She is strong but like I said, out of all my children I birthed, you were meant to be Queen. She would only become Queen in the event of your death, but without a reigning queen or general to name her, she would just be known as Lady Leader. Unless General Croz decides otherwise, which I doubt; unfortunately, they do not get along. The others will eventually find a love of their own and live their lives as citizens or continue to be your servants. Your choice, Princess."

"And me?" Princess Clarice asked.

"You what?" Queen Rae replied.

"Will I eventually find a husband of my own?" Princess Clarice asked.

Queen Rae lowered her eyes, sighed, then said, "No, my dear. You will have children to choose from for your succession but understand that love has no place in the heart of a queen. We have far more to do than to be the other half of someone's heart. Even the father of the chosen princess must be kept hidden so that royal knowledge can be passed from queen to queen without another perspective distracting the mind of the princess. It's tradition sweet girl, a hard one, but one with purpose."

Princess Clarice lowered her head, then nodded and perked up to ask her mother, "You've never approved a single thing I've done. I am so confused — why now?"

"Don't think I do not believe in your vision for our future, but I beg you to be cautious with your ambition, my princess. The survival of any colony rests on the shoulders of a dangerous thinker; they get things done. And you, my love, are our new hope. I saw that today; you're ready," Queen Rae stated. "Well now, that's done, my princess. Call for the soldiers and run this plan. Go!"

Princess Clarice gathered up the plans, humbly bowed, and smiled then left the room. She pushed Lady One and Lady Two out of the way and they fell to the ground as she stormed through the colony. Then in a powerful voice that echoed in every chamber, she shouted, "GENERAL! GENERAL!"

"Yes, Your Highness?" General Croz said as he fumbled out of the war chamber.

"Gather the soldiers — we go tonight with our plan! Go NOW!" Princess Clarice commanded as she approached the war chamber ripping the cape off and standing proudly.

"Yes, Your Highness," General Croz said as he ran toward the soldiers' chambers.

Cactus inched his way out of the war chamber with his arms folded and a proud smile. He knelt and bowed to her. Then stood up gracefully, gently grabbed her hands, and whispered in her ear, "By your side, Ricey."

Clarice smiled and Cactus released her hands and then ran to his chamber to prepare for the retrieval.

# Five

General Croz and Lieutenant Cactus gathered the twenty soldiers, supporting soldiers, and queen's ladies to prepare for the battle festival. The colony gathered under the queen's chambers to praise them for their bravery and encourage their victory. General Croz and Cactus marched to the front of the queen's podium, then Cactus announced, "Ladies and Gentleants, we are gathered tonight to begin our future! Please welcome Her Majesty Queen Rae and Her Highness Princess Clarice!"

Supporting soldiers lined up along the walls in their armor as Princess Clarice glided out of the queen's chambers in her red rose robe. Queen Rae gracefully walked out from her chambers in her long cotton purple robe and stood behind her daughter proudly. Princess Clarice nodded and grinned at her mother, winked at Cactus, then bellowed, "This is the beginning of a new day! Twenty of our brave soldiers are venturing into dangerous territory, not knowing the outcome. But here we stand ready to fight for our survival! We will live! We will survive! And we will not be conquered under this moon! We will thrive again! Soldiers march out for our mission!"

Queen Rae gleamed as the crowd roared and cheered for their brave princess. The queen's ladies lined the wall under the podium, wearing all-black hooded capes. When General Croz blew on the war horn, the soldiers formed four lines with five soldiers in each line. The ladies threw off their black capes and marched next to the soldiers in their red and black scarves, thrusting their fists into the air while they chanted:

*No living thing will conquer me!*
*No item is too big for me!*
*All ants proclaim in this colony,*
*We all will have our victory!*

The queen's ladies chanted and marched louder and louder with the soldiers to the gates of the colony. As the soldiers left, Princess Clarice removed her robe leaving her royal jewel around her neck. She graciously glided away from the honeycomb platform, arm in arm with General Croz followed by Cactus and the queen. The soldiers quietly filed out of the anthill and took their places as Queen Rae looked on and grinned proudly. As General Croz and Clarice walked out, the Scorpion Clan King Cylon cheerfully marched up to them with his lieutenant Samer.

"Your Highness, General, glad to be of assistance. The humans have been asleep for three hours now. The younger one is a light sleeper so tread softly and never near the human. My scorpions are around the perimeter, observing the young human and keeping watch for bush spiders. If this goes well, we could start rebuilding," King Cylon said excitedly. "Do you have any ants for backup just in case?"

"Of course, we do, Cylon," Queen Rae said as she emerged from the colony with a purple jewel around her neck being escorted by Cactus.

"Mother!" Princess Clarice said in shock.

Queen Rae nudged her daughter and whispered, "You didn't think I would miss your first victorious mission, did you?"

The royal pair smiled at each other, and Queen Rae directed her attention to the mission. "Our backup is awaiting my signal in the event of a crisis, but I don't foresee any problems."

King Cylon's lieutenant Samer looked into the colony as Lady Seven pushed past the backup soldiers to look out and see if her sister was all right. Samer winked at Lady Seven and confirmed the additional soldiers. King Cylon bowed to the Princess and Queen and walked away. Queen Rae rubbed her daughter's arms and smirked, whispering *'Such a delight for the stars' view'* then patted her back and sent her on her way with Cactus and another soldier.

As Princess Clarice and her aids ran away, Samer jogged up behind King Cylon and whispered, "Do you still think this is a good idea?"

"Patience, Lieutenant, we will all have what we deserve," King Cylon said as he turned and smirked at Queen Rae then started walking away to observe his soldiers.

Queen Rae watched them walk away from the corner of her eye. There was a familiar chill in the air, and it made her shudder. She remembered Cylon's words the night their oasis was destroyed, and she cowered under her bed: 'You can't hide if we are going to survive. Please, Rae, get up so we can make it.' She realized she had been hiding behind tradition all these years because she did not dare to change.

Lady Seven walked out to her mother and said, "Your Majesty, do you need anything?"

Queen Rae shook her head then turned to her daughter to say, "Seven, when it is my time to go, please make sure that her strength is greater than mine."

"Yes, Your Majesty," Lady Seven said and scurried back into the colony.

# Six

The wind was unusually strong for a desert night in the summer, but Princess Clarice, Cactus, and the two aiding soldiers ran against the desert sand that blew in their faces. She carefully jumped on the tent and flung herself into the truck. The Lieutenant and two soldiers followed and climbed up the side of the truck. She leaped through T-shirts, and towels, and finally got to the food container. The container was sealed by something hard and bendy. She pulled and pulled on it but was unable to lift it.

"Soldiers! I need assistance. What is this thing?" Princess Clarice loudly whispered.

Cactus jumped down to her and said, "It's Tupperware, Your Highness. The humans use it to store their food as we do in our colony,"

"Oh, I see," Princess Clarice said with a grin. "Ready, 1 2 3, lift!"

They all lifted the lid with all their might and then smiled when the juicy watermelon was revealed. The soldiers positioned themselves to pass the fruit down to the line of soldiers that had huddled under the truck. Princess Clarice began handing the pieces of fruit to the soldiers who threw them down to the line. Cactus stopped for a moment, put his arm around Clarice, and smirked. She smiled back and asked, "What is it?"

"You've saved us all. We'll figure out what to do after this is gone, don't you worry. There will be more; we got this. Let's do it, Your *Majesty*."

Princess Clarice grinned, and hugged Cactus then turned her attention back to the mission. They pushed out the fifth and sixth pieces of fruit and suddenly, there was a bellowing noise, and the ground was shaking. They fell over in the truck and covered their ears, but it barely silenced the noise. The youngest human had been stabbed by a scorpion and shook the ground while he let out a shrill scream and stomped out of the tent.

"Now that's a sound I know!" King Cylon evilly cackled.

The queen held her head trying to deafen the human's scream as they ran around and shook the ground in their panicked steps.

"Beta team, go, go, go! Queen's Guard, secure my daughter and cover the colony!" Queen Rae commanded.

The soldiers charged toward the scorpions. As the humans watched the scorpion and ant armies get near them, they began stomping and smashing some of the scorpions and ants. The ant soldiers ran away from the humans, but some of the scorpions cornered them, forcing them back toward the stomping humans.

Princess Clarice and her companions stumbled and climbed to the top of the truck. When they reached the door, they watched as a horrific battle unfolded with scorpions and ants flying through the air and smashing into the sand, while others fought to save the colony. Some tried to fight away the scorpion's stinger but became weak and got stabbed. Ten soldiers climbed onto the truck and yelled for the princess. Cactus tried to wrap his arms around Clarice to pull her out, but she pushed him away.

"Get out of here!" Princess Clarice commanded.

"Prin..." Cactus stuttered.

"I said go! That's an order, Lieutenant. Secure the colony," Princess Clarice commanded.

"Ricey! I promised you—" Cactus scolded.

"This is not about me. Go! Go, soldier!" Princess Clarice commanded.

Cactus and his companion reluctantly jumped down from the truck. He drew both his swords; he ran furiously toward their enemies, chopping every scorpion leg and flipping to avoid spikes and following up with slicing the enemy's weapon off to clear the way for the princess to run. He turned to look back toward the truck and whispered,

"Come on, Ricey. Come on." He continued to fight as two other soldiers yelled up to the princess.

"Princess, climb down to us!"

"We must get you back to the colony!"

Clarice was terrified into stiffness by what she saw. She saw Cactus fighting to clear a way for her and General Croz shouting orders and cutting down any scorpion in his path. One tear streamed down her face as she looked in despair over at her mother in the distance. Her mother kept a stiff lip, stared back at her daughter, then nodded and mouthed '*Be strong*'. The glance between them distracted Queen Rae from King Cylon swinging his tail around and stabbing at her.

"You think your colony is the only one that needs food in this desert!" King Cylon yelled as he tried to strike her again.

The queen flipped over his tail and avoided his strike, then yelled, "The only one worthy!"

"No!" Princess Clarice yelled as she leaped off the truck, stumbled, and rolled onto the ground, then sprinted toward her mother.

Queen Rae kept leaping over King Cylon's tail and strikes. A soldier rushed her quartz sword with a handle that was adorned in the multicolored stones of the desert up to her from the colony. Queen Rae swung the sword above her head as Cylon charged at her with his stinger. His menace endured the strikes of the sword and he kept charging toward her to strike down the queen. With every swing and strike of their battle, Princess Clarice ran faster and faster through battle circles cutting off the legs of the enemies and jumping over spike strikes.

Before Clarice could reach the queen, a scorpion snatched her by the legs and hung her on their stinger. Cactus saw her hanging on the stinger and quickly began cutting and running towards her, to help. When the scorpion tried to smash her into the cold sand, the ground vibrated as a panicking human ran up and kicked the scorpion through the air.

Princess Clarice flew up in the air and away from her mother. Queen Rae shrieked believing Clarice was dead as she disappeared into the night sky. Cactus and General Croz let out rage-filled screams and ran toward the princess with their swords drawn. Clarice's attacker hit a rock and died instantly while she landed on a tumbleweed. She rolled around in the tumbleweed and eventually slipped off onto the ground, face planting into the sand. Her arms shook as she pushed herself back up and stumbled back to the ground panting and crying.

Meanwhile, the queen's sorrow turned to rage, and she swung her sword above her head and scraped it against the sand setting it ablaze. She charged toward Cylon and gave one final flaming blow to his gut and let out a bellowing growl and scream. The humans drove off and all in battle stopped and stared at Queen Rae. The scorpions stared somberly at their leader and scurried away from the ants with Lieutenant Samer. The Queen stood in front of him with pride as he lay dying in the cold sand. Princess Clarice looked on from the distance and smiled at her victorious mother. Cactus saw his friend walking back to them in the distance and hunched over in relief and started walking towards the Queen. Clarice called out, "Majesty! Mommy! I'm here. We did it!"

Princess Clarice started to run back toward her mother, joyfully ignoring her war scars. Queen Rae turned around and smiled then dropped her sword to open her arms for her daughter. Suddenly, King Cylon used his last strength to strike the queen through her back with his stinger. Clarice shrieked and sprinted toward her mother. Cactus was horrified into silence and started running towards the Queen. General Croz ragefully shrieked with tears in his eyes and ran to her aid. The queen fell next to the dying scorpion and said with a heavy breath, "Cylon, how could you? We are your allies; you were my friend. We've been in this place together for over fifty crescents. Your colony needs food, and you fight us for it. We were going to share as we've always done. But now you leave nothing but a legacy of disgrace and no one left to lead your colony."

"Friends don't let other friends starve. My father was right about you. I finally did what my father couldn't and defeated you like the pest you are. My legacy is your defeat. It doesn't matter what comes next! My colony won!" Cylon snarled in his final breaths.

"Yes, but unlike your monsters, we will survive," Queen Rae said on her final breath.

The two leaders closed their eyes and died. Princess Clarice, the General, and Cactus finally reached Rae's side. The princess collapsed over her, letting out a piercing scream. The queen lay with her arms spread out and her head held high as the soldiers crowded around her solemnly. The General held his tears back, picked up the queen, and carried her into the colony followed by soldiers. Princess Clarice toppled over and uncontrollably sobbed grabbing her chest as if to grasp the pain in her entire body. Cactus withheld his tears, picked her up, and carried her back to her chambers. While soldiers whispered about him breaking royal protocol by the way he handled the princess, he ignored them and kept whispering to the princess *'You are the strongest warrior this colony has ever known.'*

The next morning, Queen Rae was placed on a large stone in the center of the colony. She was wrapped from head to toe in purple and white silk, with her crown placed on her stomach. The entire colony surrounded her, and silently weeping soldiers lined the walls of the colony. Princess Clarice walked down to the stone in a long, hooded, fuchsia and gold cape, knitted from cotton. General Croz stood at the head of the queen and Cactus stood at her feet, both holding their swords diagonally across their armored chests. Cactus stared at his friend trying to keep it together and quivered in his sadness. The queen's ladies followed behind Clarice in hooded, black and gold, beaded, cotton knit capes, and rocked back and forth humming the song of mourning and Lady One began to sing:

*They say every star must take its place,*
*among the night sky where it was once day.*

Princess Clarice continued along with her sister.

*Even in the dark, we can see,*
*the hope of tomorrow because you shine so brightly.*

The rest of the colony joined in on the song.

*And you will shine on us, shine on us, Majesty.*
*Keep on shining on us, shining on us our queen.*

*And you will shine on us, shine on us, Majesty.*
*Keep on shining on us, shining on us our queen.*

They surrounded the stone and dropped to their knees as Princess Clarice walked up to view her mother's body. She never imagined that this would be how she ascended to Queen. Traditionally, her mother would have crowned her and there would be a great celebration. She thought back to when she had just turned ten crescents and she and her mother danced in the queen's chambers playfully rehearsing for her coronation dance. After tossing scarves and robes around, she lifted her and said, "I will always dance in the shadow of your glory."

Clarice removed her hood and kissed her mother on her wrapped forehead, then whispered, "By your choice and command, I will lead this colony to greatness. I love you, Mom."

Lady Seven and Lady Eight stepped up to the platform and removed the princess' cape. Lady Seven placed her cape over the queen's body while Lady Eight removed the crown. Lady Ten then stepped up to the platform and helped Lady Seven put their mother's royal purple and gold cape onto Princess Clarice. Then, in unison, the three ladies placed the crown on top of her head and bowed as they backed down from the stone. In a rippling motion, the queen's ladies removed their mourning capes and revealed yellow celebration capes for their sister, the new queen.

Queen Clarice looked around at the crowd as each ant and Queen's ladies kneeled before her. She stood firmly by her mother's body and lifted her head to watch the sunlight peek through the top of the colony and hide her quivering breath. She stretched out her arms and closed her eyes as the sunlight caressed her face and shined on her mother, soldiers, and the colony. The general and lieutenant clanked their swords above their new queen and led their crowd in unison to say, "All hail, Queen Clarice!"

# Seven

The colony was hauntingly silent with few echoes of small rocks and children running through the hollowed tubes. The retrieved fruit was scattered on the battlefield and what made it to the colony was divided among the hundreds of ants. All that was left was a single black seed that was carried to Queen Clarice's chamber. Queen Rae was buried in the royal crypt and her grave was covered in black smooth shiny pebbles called obsidian; it was taught by the Scorpion clan that those stones kept the energy of royals in the colony to protect it. Queen Clarice asked for no celebrations for her ascension. Normally, allies and the colony would celebrate under the crescent moon with a brilliant song and dance that could shake the stars awake and force them to shine upon the new reign. Instead, the new queen restlessly lay in her new chamber with guilt over her mother's death as the moon slowly changed from a waning crescent into a new moon cycle. The sun had twenty chances to warm the colony, but every sunset led to a night that got colder and colder.

During one of those solemn days, Cactus paced around the war chamber wondering how the retrieval could've gone right. He looked over the plans, and historical documents that would have hinted at the ambush, but there was nothing that could have prepared them for this great loss. He grunted and snarled as he tossed the documents all over the war chamber, then finally collapsed to the ground and screamed in anger.

\*\*\*

General Croz sat in his chambers and sobbed himself into a deep slumber, then would awaken and cry more. One day he stopped his sob as he held a piece of Rae's princess crown then clutched it and he said, "At least we still have Clarice, but Rae you will always be my princess."

Suddenly Lady One prances into General Croz's chambers and clears her throat to get his attention. He mumbled, "Ugh nightshade."

"The proper soldier time for mourning is one day, General. It is time for you to get up and get these soldiers in shape for their new orders. Do you hear me? I said get up!" Lady One scolded and Croz rolled his eyes and glared at her, "Daddy! Get up! You're embarrassing me!"

"I am no more your father than you are the next queen. Get out One. I'll get up when I'm ready." General Croz grumbled then laid back down.

Lady One huffed and marched out of the General's chamber.

Lady Seven, Eight, Nine, and Seventeen lay on the bed in their sister's old room, staring up at the honeycomb in grave stillness as they worried about their queen and colony.

Lady Eight abruptly sat up and broke the silence, "I wasn't expecting her to take over until her twentieth crescent celebration. Isn't that the tradition?"

"Usually, it's up to the queen. Mother became Queen at her eighteenth crescent, but I think it was coming soon anyway given her leadership on this fruit thing," Lady Nine explained as she folded her arms and then continued in her frustration. "She needs to get out of that room and do something. We're still starving!"

Lady Seventeen sat up, sighed, and said, "Are we going to get our own lives now? Does she still want us to serve her as we served our mother? Don't get me wrong, I'm devastated. But she hasn't come out of Mother's room, and the new moon is nearly finished! No telling what she's thinking, least of all about us. She's only a girl eighteen crescents!"

Lady Seven stood up angrily and turned to her sisters. "Nineteen! Nineteen crescents tomorrow! Like any of you care though! Do you know why she slept under the honeycomb her whole life?" They all nodded and Lady Seven scolded, "She knows it, too. Every queen has had the opportunity to watch their successor take over and guide them. Our sister has been robbed of that. Her first major mission took our mother, and she has the weight of the colony on her shoulders, yet you sit here questioning her leadership and wondering about your own lives! We sleep under this honeycomb too for a reason! Our mother is gone, but we are here to support our queen until dismissed. Trust her, trust our queen and be the ladies you were raised to be."

Meanwhile, Clarice finally arose from her bed and sauntered over to the seed in her chamber and stared at it. Her growing rage finally burst out, and she began to beat it.

"It wasn't worth it! It wasn't worth it! All of this for what? For what?" Queen Clarice exclaimed and cried.

She sobbed and laid up against the seed still trying to beat it as if it would undo the past. As her tears calmed, she laid back down on the bed with a shaky breath and tried to focus on being the new queen.

In the queen's ladies' chambers gleeful melodies irritatingly echoed through the walls. Lady One danced around her chambers joyfully and played around with the scarves, pretending they were different robes, happily waiting for her sister to give up the crown. She tauntingly sang,

*It's all mine.*
*Hallowed caverns are ripe for control.*
*Feed me, love me, adore me,*
*I rule —*
*you kingdom of fools.*
*Give it time,*
*it's all mine.*

Lady Two watched her with equal excitement with a plastered smile but was annoyed by her overzealous celebration. Still, she hoped that she'd be put in place of authority when Lady One would become Queen. Just as she was about to speak on her desires, Cactus marched in and glared at Lady One.

"You seem very joyful considering your mother just died," Cactus said.

"That may be. But I know my *sweet* little baby sister is not up for this task and I am next in line. General Croz said so. She's a sniveling piece of spoiled trash that had no place in my colony from the beginning. So, when she tosses the crown, this is all mine," Lady One joyfully explained as she continued to skip around.

Lady Two popped up, grabbed a scarf, and started to playfully spin, mimicking Lady One.

"I don't want her up on that throne any more than you do. She's been ill-prepared and thwarted by us for years. What wouldn't stop her now? Remember when she tried to build a new chamber for the children and we broke all the walls so it would collapse," Lady Two evilly cackled then continued. "When you are Queen, dear sister, you take care of me, and I will keep these miserable gullible ants in line."

Cactus drew his sword and shouted, "How dare you! Not only do you speak against our queen but your sister!"

Lady One sashayed over to Cactus, lowered his sword, and cupped his face, then said, "When I am Queen, you and your little crush will be out in the desert for the bush spiders to feed. Unless you want to be my general."

"Ugh," Cactus said as he backed away from her in disgust. He continued to back out of their chambers and said, "You have no place in this family or colony, and I will personally see to it that my queen is protected from you."

Cactus angrily stomped through the colony and marched into Queen Clarice's chamber. He saw her sitting on the floor and slowed his march to a calm step. He carefully inched his way to her, sat down on the floor, and said, "Your Majesty. *Riiiceeey...*"

"Get out of here, Cactus," Queen Clarice snapped.

"Your Majesty, I know you didn't want a celebration, but your next crescent is tomorrow and it's time for your first proclamation," Cactus calmly stated.

"You do it then! My mother is dead; I don't know what I'm doing! All because we were starving, and I tried to find a way out of it! Now everything is destroyed! Don't you get it! This is our life; this is how it ends!" Queen Clarice whined.

"Clarice!" Cactus bellowed.

"You do not address me without title, Lieutenant!" Queen Clarice snapped.

"Oh good, so you are still planning on being Queen. So now what? You sit in here and sulk about your first mistake. Sure, it was big, but that is the price of greatness. Living in this colony is a constant battle but we all still get up and fight!" Cactus said firmly.

"Anthony! Don't you dare—" Clarice interjected.

"Dare what? Tell you that we need our queen or demand that you honor your birthright. You're my queen, but you're also my best friend, Ricey.

I'm not going to allow you to stop your progress because you made one mistake. I love you and that's it," Cactus passionately explained.

"Queens can't marry," Clarice blurted out.

Cactus was confused and said, "That was random."

"I love you too, but we can't be married," Queen Clarice stated.

Cactus took a solemn breath and calmly said, "Well, you're Queen now; you can make that choice. In the meantime, I'll make sure you have your space until you figure out how you want to lead us." Cactus left the royal chamber and mumbled, "Sun, moon, and stars help us."

On the morning of her 19th crescent, she walked out of the heavy oak door where no one stood to protect or greet her. She aimlessly walked through the colony that continued to sound hollow and lifeless. Without announcement, she climbed out of the colony and sat at the gates looking out toward the rising sun. The slaughtered ants and scorpions still littered the ground. Queen Clarice looked up towards the sky and closed her eyes trying to think of what to do next. Suddenly, a sphinx moth swooped down and grabbed her. The moth took off into the air while Queen Clarice struggled to get free from its clutches.

"What are you doing? Unhand me! Let me go, you desert beast! That's an order!" Queen Clarice screamed.

The moth was silent and flew forward toward the sun. Queen Clarice eventually fell limp in the clutch of the moth. Then she was dropped onto a leaf and awakened by the reflection of the shining sun from dew. She sat up and gasped at the ornate view decorated with giant trees, tall grass, fragrant flowers, and most importantly water.

Suddenly she remembered something General Croz told her on her eighth crescent celebration. He sat on the floor with her as she played with the gifts that her sisters made smiled and said,

"You know my little princess, some time ago this colony was surrounded by bushes, grass, trees, cactus, and other beautiful plants. Maybe one day you can help us get it all back."

Young Clarice scrunched up her face and stuttered through her confidence, "No-no way! That's a fairytale Croz! This is a desert, and this is how it's supposed to be. The bees were our friends a long-long time ago and gave us honeycomb an-an-and the scorpions look out for us, and my mommy-the queen — she takes care of us like all the other queens. There is no such thing as what you're talking about."

General Croz chuckled and said, "All right Princess, maybe one day you'll see that this world doesn't have to be this way."

Queen Clarice shouted, "It's real!" and enthusiastically jumped down and began running through the grass amazed at the beautiful giant flowers as she made her way to a stream. She drank water and ate small pieces of different fruits that grew from the trees. She playfully ran through this strange land and smiled at the beauty; she spun around and then, suddenly, hesitation for her joy overcame her because she feared this was a vivid dream or mirage of some kind.

She collapsed onto a nearby fallen leaf and watched the sky, as the sun began to paint the sky orange and pink before revealing the twinkle and light of the moon and stars. The moth glided down to her leaf as the twilight reflected off of the emerald strapped onto his body with four strands of woven gold. Queen Clarice quickly sat up and before she could ask about where she was, he said in a deep mellow tone,

"I am Larry, King of the Sphinx Moths. May I have permission to speak, Your Majesty?"

Queen Clarice jumped up and gasped then trembled as she tiptoed towards the king. She bowed and then said, "You are a fellow leader — please address me as Clarice. Forgive me, Larry, but I was told you were dead. All your clan fled or died off after the bush spider attack."

King Larry sadly nodded and said, "I was still a young royal caterpillar, eight crescents old when the bush spiders attacked. We huddled in your mother's old room. Cylon was the bravest of us. He stood ready to fight as we cowered under the bed. By the order of the royal families, we were all to be carried away to safety. Ayo and I were taken first by the soldiers of my clan, but when they returned for Cylon and your mother, they were killed. When I grew my wings, I flew back to come and lead your mother and Cylon here, but they wanted to rebuild their colonies on shattered ground. So, they kept their treaty and sent me away."

Queen Clarice scowled and huffed, "King Cylon attacked us! He broke our treaty after generations of protecting us! He swore he was an ally but turned on us because he was desperate for power!"

King Larry nestled himself next to Clarice. "I know. Word traveled about the ambush. Shock does not begin to describe my feelings but mostly, I am disappointed. His father did not raise him to be a monster, but his circumstances turned him into one. I'm sorry he turned on you — that was not the brother we knew."

Queen Clarice turned to face King Larry and whispered through halted tears, "Why have you brought me here?"

Suddenly, the hum of three bees surrounded them and Queen Ayo gracefully fluttered down. Her head was adorned with woven beeswax and jewels collected from the oasis. She gracefully walked towards Queen Clarice, one foot in front of the other as if preparing to dance. She stopped in front of Clarice, placed her hand on her stomach, bowed, and said, "Your Majesty. At last, we meet. I am Queen Ayo of the Oasis Bees. Welcome home." She snapped back up, put her hand on her hip, sassily leaned to the side, and said, "We need your ants, girl."

The three royals began to casually walk through the abundant oasis as Queen Ayo told the story of rebuilding the joint oasis kingdom. When Larry and Ayo fled the old oasis, the soldiers had no idea where to go. They found a dying oasis and dropped them there.

The bush spiders attacked because they wanted the land and none of its inhabitants, but after they tore it apart and only the ants were left to run it, the land quickly fell apart and died. The bush spiders wandered the desert growing in fury and looped the scorpions into that fury then attacked the ants again for what little they had because they didn't want to work for it.

"They would rather attack, pillage, and claim than be a part of our community and work the land. Mala is a fifth-generation descendant of a bitter, lazy, angry species. That hate has been fermenting for five generations, sweet Sun!

"Was there ever a time they had their own?" Queen Clarice asked.

"They only had what they took. They won't come here though," Queen Ayo said.

"Why? They're bigger than all of us," Queen Clarice asked.

"There's more of us together than them alone. And this time, we're ready for a fight. Their selfish ways have started to dwindle their species, and now, they steal out of fear, survival, and pure greed that served them so well for generations. They come here — they won't survive the ambush... plus, we can fly," King Larry stated.

"Clarice, you must bring your ants here. You will be able to plant your seed and grow hundreds of watermelons and other food here in this oasis. The colony will flourish and be safe. I tried to talk Rae into coming here, but she wanted to respect the traditions of the queens before her," Queen Ayo said somberly.

"She was strong on tradition, but she believed in me. But my colony will not believe me. I heard their groans and remarks about my mother's death being my fault. I'm better off staying here, alone," Queen Clarice said somberly.

"You would live here alone, with no one to rule or keep you company all because of one mistake?" King Larry asked.

"It was a big mistake! I cannot make this better! I'm not ready for this," Queen Clarice shouted.

"Yes, Your Majesty, but who else could they possibly listen to?" King Larry stated.

Queen Clarice shrugged and asked, "How did you know about the seed?"

"When you fly high, you can see everything and make better decisions. I have been waiting for you to come out of that chamber and stop living in your guilt. Don't waste more time memorializing what you can't get back when there is so much to look forward to," King Larry said.

Before Clarice could speak another word, King Larry picked her up and took off back toward the colony. As they flew over the desert Clarice looked down at the barren land with small areas covered in different types of cacti, tumbleweed, and lovegrass. She asked King Larry why anyone would choose to live in an environment like this. He explained that a desert is a place between an ending and a new beginning. Some of the old things remain, because they still serve a purpose, while graciously giving space for all the new possibilities to come. To be a part of the possibilities to come is the greatest adventure anyone could ask for.

# Eight

Lady Seven walked through the colony and hummed an old lullaby their mother would sing to them. *'No matter the joy, no matter the sorrow, here we are. Here we are. Here we are.'* It hauntingly echoed through all the chambers as she walked towards Queen Clarice's hallway. She got to the oakwood door and saw it was ajar. She knocked and it inched open. As she cautiously tiptoed into the royal chamber, she heard singing and cheerfully jogged into the bedroom... And she saw her sister, Lady One, spinning and dancing and trying on Clarice's crown and cape.

"One! What in the stars are you doing in here? Are you crazy? You'll be banished!" Lady Seven scolded.

Lady One slowly turned around as the cape draped around her and she said in a snide, calm voice, "Seven... Nice of you to join me. Although I prefer to be called Até. The name has always suited me. Queen Até, the one who saved the colony after the mistakes of royalty — Rae, and Clarice — nearly drove us to death."

She sauntered towards her infuriated sister then pet her face and continued, "You've always been a loyal servant. I'll keep you. But the others can be lost to the desert for all I care."

Lady Seven smacked away Lady One's hand and shouted, "Queen Clarice is not dead! The general would never appoint you, Queen! A queen leads for all; you lead for glory. Guards!"

Lieutenant Cactus and royal guards ran towards the royal chamber. Lady One snatched off the robe and crown and threw them onto the bed to avoid the guards from seeing her with them. Lady Seven sneered at Lady One, grabbed her throat, and menacingly whispered, "Where is my sister? What did you do to her?"

Lady One struggled to breathe, but her callous heart encouraged her to speak. "I don't know, I guess she left. This is my colony now and you're banished."

Cactus and the royal guard ran into the chambers and Lady Seven let go of her sister. Lady One theatrically tried to catch her breath and cried to the guards, "We can't find her." She whined and gasped as she collapsed to her knees, "We came in here to check on her and saw she threw her crown and robe on the bed. No telling where she could be! Please, please find her."

Cactus and Lady Seven rolled their eyes as the royal guard was captivated by the performance, with her ending hunched over on her knees crying. The soldiers nodded and ran off to start the search for their queen. Lady One began to catch her breath and sit up from her dramatic act. As soon as she raised her head, Lady Seven punched her in the face and her legs flipped up as she flew toward the wall.

"Seven!" Cactus shouted authoritatively as he marched toward an ailing Lady One. "Nice hit."

"I've been waiting for twenty-three crescents to do that." Lady Seven crouched down to her sister's face. "You may be the oldest, but you have the least sense. You've never been good enough to be loved, let alone be queen. But this I can do for you… *My sister.*"

Lady Seven grabbed Lady One's legs and slowly dragged her out of the royal chambers. Cactus smirked at their enemy's humiliation, but he was overcome with worry about Clarice and set out to find her.

\*\*\*

Meanwhile, the general, the queen's ladies, and the rest of the colony were in a panic as they all searched for their queen.

Some of the queen's ladies stood by the queen's chamber and watched the chaos. They worriedly whispered amongst themselves until Lady One limped her way to them, adjusted herself to mimic a royal stance, and interrupted, "Ladies, do not panic. Queen Rae being the great mother and queen she was, said that I am to be appointed Queen if Clarice proved to be unfit. She has obviously abandoned the colony. Or better yet, wandered into the desert and died," she cackled wickedly.

"How dare you speak so dreadfully of our sister. We already lost our mother; we do not need to lose our sister too," Lady Eight stated firmly.

"Once I am officially appointed Queen by the general, you will be the first to be banished... Dear sister," Lady One softly scolded.

Just then a soldier came running into the colony yelling, "The queen approaches! She is flying in!"

"FLYING?" the colony turned and said in unison.

Queen Clarice descended gracefully into the colony with the last kiss of sunlight touching the gates and the tips of King Larry's wings. He dropped her down and she looked kindly amongst her ants, as everyone stood and stared in shock. She knew that she made a mistake, but also knew that she made a promise to lead the colony. She took a deep breath and then strutted down into the colony while four Queen's ladies and guards rushed to her sides. Cactus pushed and shoved past all of them in the crowd and grabbed the queen by the hand and bowed.

"Your Majesty, we were worried. Do you need assistance?" Cactus asked out of breath.

"No, I'm fine. Thank you for your concern. Gather everyone beneath my chambers for an announcement. It's time to change our lives today," Queen Clarice said as she winked at Cactus. He popped up from his stooping position and ordered the soldiers to gather the colony beneath the Queen's chambers.

Queen Clarice emerged from her chambers in her radiant purple and gold robe and was escorted by three soldiers, Cactus, and the general. She requested that all the queen's ladies gather in the front and all the soldiers surrounded the colony. The crowd anxiously awaited her words and some shook in their knees. She walked up to the edge of the ledge and bellowed.

"I am grateful and humbled by your concern. I come before you today to tell you that the very way we live is changing at this moment. My first royal decree is to eliminate all controversy in my close quarters. As of this moment and forevermore, Lady One and Lady Two, you are stripped of your titles and numbers. Guards! Bring them up to me."

The crowd gasped and nervously chattered as the other queen's ladies unanimously stepped away from their tarnished sisters. Two soldiers grabbed the former ladies as Lady Two's knees buckled as she was dragged up to the queen, sobbing and inaudibly screaming at Lady One. However, Lady One scowled at Queen Clarice as she gracefully stepped up to the royal balcony. As Lady Two continued to sob, Lady One hauntingly whispered to her little sister, "I suppose this is the end. Understand, baby sister, even in my death I will be greater than you."

Queen Clarice whispered back, "Death is a graciousness you two do not deserve." She snatched off their royal scarves, turned the crowd, and bellowed, "My disgraced sisters have plotted against my reign my entire life, a crime punishable by death." Queen Clarice turned toward her sisters and slyly smirked then continued, "Until today. You will no longer participate in any royal matters of the colony and work as an aid to our soldiers. Unless General Croz is generous enough to name you, you will only be worth your labor and the most disposable among us."

The crowd was stunned and anxiously murmured among themselves while the disgraced ladies shook in anger and fear. Queen Clarice turned back to the crowd and said, "As of today, I am disbanding the queen's ladies, and my loyal sisters will be free to work as they choose, marry whomever they want or not marry, and have lives of their own."

The queen's ladies jumped and cheered and cried tears of joy. Queen Clarice looked to Lieutenant Cactus, and he nodded for her approval of the next order. She continued, "For the disgraces that stand before you, they too can marry anyone brave enough to have them. And, if they should have children, they will live as my loyal subjects and not bear the mark of disgrace that their mothers carry. No child should suffer  for what wrongdoing their parents have done."

"Moons and stars! Queen Mother would never allow this! This is a new day," former Lady Seven shouted among her sisters.

Take them away and put them to work," Queen Clarice ordered.

She shooed them away and turned to face her colony. The guards pulled the disgraces away and suddenly, Lady One broke free from the soldiers' grip, lunged at the queen, and shouted, "You will be the greatest shame this colony has ever seen! Our true queen died in vain because of you. She should have left you for dead and appointed me, a true leader!"

Queen Clarice stood calmly and faced the colony, as Lieutenant Cactus marched over to Lady One, pulled his sword on her, and roared, "You were never meant to be Queen, servant! It is your sister's grace that has spared your life, a quality you have never had! But under my watch and my soldiers' care, you will have no such leniency." He sheathed his sword and continued, "Take them away, soldiers."

The lieutenant took his place at the side of the queen as she glanced among her ants and noticed their anxious faces. She raised her hands as if to hug the colony and bellowed, "Today, we end our days of sorrow and take steps toward days of triumph! I woke up this morning and sat at the top of our colony then looked at the faces of our fallen soldiers. I will admit, I thought it was hopeless. Then I was taken to a wonderful place, an oasis, where we could rebuild our lives. Now, as your queen, I am asking you to trust me. I am not angry at those who fear this new beginning because I feel the same way. As it was said by our first Queen Carrie: 'We cannot be afraid to try.' General, please bring forward the seed."

General Croz and four soldiers carried the watermelon seed and placed it next to her. She grabbed hold of the seed along with the other soldiers and happily looked it over. The crowd whispered in curiosity and pointed up at the seed. Queen Clarice cleared her throat and said, "This is all that remains of our war — one watermelon seed. When we plant it in the oasis, it can only create one watermelon. I know it sounds foolish to put all our hope in one watermelon. But the one watermelon will have hundreds more seeds that will be planted and create hundreds upon hundreds of more watermelons. We will not live underground; we will live under the kind shade next to gentle flowing water and an abundance of food. This is the beautiful future that I see for our colony. I will be your honest queen and tell you that our path there will not be easy, but we will get there with strength and belief in the future."

The crowd was silent and stared up at the queen. She panned the crowd and saw their doubtful faces. Worry overcame her strong heart and she wondered if she was making another mistake. One citizen bravely blurted out, "The last time you had an idea like this half our soldiers were killed and our queen! We need to get back to our traditions and get this colony in line!"

Lieutenant Cactus began to draw his sword, but the queen raised her hand to halt him, took a deep breath, and bellowed with power, "We have been here for many crescents, and it was paradise for some time. Traditions were once new ideas that everyone liked, so we kept doing them. Those traditions were never intended to destroy us for the sake of honoring what was once a good idea. Soldiers, past generals, and citizens did not fight, dig, scavenge, and live just for us to be in this moment and starve! We must move on. And we will carry the history with us, mount it on a hill for all to remember, while we dance in the present and celebrate the days to come. I call upon all the stars that after we plant this one seed future leaders will be wise enough to create new ideas that will continue to prosper us. The thriving life of our descendants depends on our courage to say yes now."

The crowd was silent again. Suddenly, a small group of children began to clap, then another group clapped, then another clapped and cheered. Soon, the entire colony was cheering; Clarice's heart was once again filled with hope.

# Nine

Queen Clarice immediately ordered that everyone pack only what is necessary and meaningful and prepare to leave in three days. After she disbanded the queen's ladies, she named ten of her loyal sisters to be on her royal court.

Lady Seven, now Jasmine, served as head of the queen's council. She was joined by her newly named sisters Dylan, Daphne, and Helena. Lady Seventeen, now Noelle, served as the leader of the royal aides that performed necessary tasks for the move and construction of the new colony; her sisters Marie, Jessie, and Dora joined her.

As ordered, the citizens gathered only what they could carry on their backs and two days later, they were ready to leave. Lieutenant Cactus ordered soldiers to pack up ancient scrolls and crowns of past queens so they may carry their history with them. The royal aides had groups of fifty walking out with twenty soldiers as an escort.

Queen Clarice stood in the colony wrapped in her purple royal robe and reminisced about her life. She paced slowly with her mother's robe tapping her feet and could hear the echoes of songs sung by her mother and memories of the love shared. She glanced at the glimmering gates in the sunlight and watched as the last group of ants walked out for the last time. Then, soldiers carried the watermelon seed out, and she fully accepted and smiled at their new hope.

"Your Majesty, are you ready to leave?" Council Dylan asked as Jasmine and Marie ran up behind her.

Queen Clarice turned around with a grin, removed her purple robe, and said, "Council Dylan, please tell two guards to wait for me in here. The rest of the court must leave now," Queen Clarice said.

"Your Majesty, Sister, why have you removed your robe?" Jasmine asked.

"I am leaving some of our mother's traditions here where she is being left, starting with this robe," Queen Clarice said.

"How will the colony identify you as Queen?" organizer Marie asked.

"They know my face. Plus, I would never give up my crown and those fabulous scarves." Queen Clarice laughed.

Queen Clarice walked through the hallowed halls of the old colony carrying the heavy royal robe and hearing the whispers of wind through the different chambers. She passed by her mother's grave and laid her hand upon the obsidian pebbles and whispered *see you later*. She walked back to the royal oak door and glanced around Queen Rae's elaborate room. She unfolded her robe and laid it across the bed. Without hesitation, she quickly turned and left her home.

The colony stood outside watching the sunset as Queen Clarice walked out. Unfortunately, the remains of the gruesome battle still littered the desert. While some were uneasy because of the sights surrounding them, Queen Clarice encouraged them by yelling, "March toward the light."

They walked for five hours into the cooling desert. Many of them were feeling the unbearable cold for the first time and chattered enough to make the items on their backs rattle. Some insisted on stopping for the night, but the court, Cactus, and General advised the queen that it would be too dangerous. They continued for three more hours under the faintly lit stars and waxing crescent moon until the groans from the tired children, soldiers, and a weary royal court made them agree to stop for the night.

They came upon a collection of tumbleweed and Queen Clarice decided to stop and set up a camp for the remainder of the night. The soldiers and some court members wove the tumbleweed into a fence and surrounded the colony. Queen Clarice and her royal court gathered together, and

Council Jasmine asked, "Your Majesty, are you sure you know where you are going?"

"Not to question your judgment, but how do we even know if this seed you have asked us to carry will work in this new land?" Council Noelle asked.

"Sisters, I understand your concern. And to be honest, I know the general direction of where we must go. I don't know if the watermelon seed will work or not. But I know this land is fruitful and we will survive regardless. I needed to give them hope; they have been hopeless for so long," Queen Clarice explained.

"Your Majesty, what about our protection tonight? Even though we have the tumbleweed around us, we are defenseless out here," General Croz said.

"And, not to mention, everyone is freezing," Aid Marie stated.

"Well, what do you suggest?" Queen Clarice asked

"I have a suggestion!" Council Daphne shouted. Everyone turned and looked at her as she stood up from amongst the crowd and said, "Your Majesty, Court, and ants, we need to huddle together to keep warm, then the soldiers can use their spears to create fires with the tumbleweed. It will keep away attackers and we will stay warm until dawn."

Queen Clarice shrugged and smirked, then said, "Let's do it!"

Everyone inched into a huddle while the fires were lit and placed around the camp. Queen Clarice sat in the middle and laughed and talked to her ants about the new colony. General Croz put his arm around Clarice and said, "You're doing great, my queen."

"General...Da-Daddy?" Queen Clarice stuttered. With tears welling in his eyes, he nodded, and she continued, "Why was it a tradition to number my sisters instead of giving them a name? They're all special in their own way."

General Croz sighed and said, "Well sweetheart, any ant born of from a queen had to compete to be worthy. It's a stupid tradition. I'm glad you stopped it."

They both joyfully chuckled and Clarice said, "I know queens couldn't marry, but we couldn't have a father? We need you too. I needed you."

General Croz put his arm around Clarice and hugged her and said, "Rules and roles aside I have always been your father and will always be by your side."

Clarice wiped a joyful tear from her eye and asked, "Croz, I don't even know your name."

"Will! Will Croz is my name," General Croz stated gleefully.

Jasmine sashayed up to the leaders, motioned to politely interrupt the father and daughter, then pulled Queen Clarice aside and said, "Sister, I know it's none of my business, but why do you call the Lieutenant, Cactus?"

"When we were young, he was assigned as my only friend and although he hated it, he would go on adventures with me. One day, we came up to a cactus and while I was amazed, he was unimpressed and had a shield up about him. But then, we kept climbing into the cactus and found the sweet juice inside. After that, he finally started talking to me. And since I didn't know his name at the time, I started to call him Cactus. Prickly on the outside, but once you get past that, he's sweet."

Council Helena scuttled up to the sisters and interrupted, "He loves you. Will our sister have her king?"

Queen Clarice sighed. "Queens are not allowed to marry. It's a distraction."

Council Jasmine said, "Well, doesn't a queen have a say over her own life?"

Clarice looked over at Jasmine and smiled.

Just as Clarice was about to respond, Cactus walked up to the sisters and cleared his throat.

"Your Majesty, Council, and Aid. We're finally settled in. How are you feeling?" Lieutenant Cactus said formally.

"Very well, Lieutenant, considering it's chilly out here," Queen Clarice answered softly.

The friends fought their affections for one another and exchanged coy glances until Cactus smirked and playfully nodded to suggest that they take a walk. The queen and Lieutenant strolled and traced the perimeter around the colony silently as her sisters delightfully gazed at them. Clarice was bashful and Cactus boldly but gently grabbed her hand.

"Cactus?" Clarice shyly called his name.

"Yeah, Ricey," Cactus replied.

"Do you think you could be king?" Clarice asked.

Cactus grinned, chuckled, and asked, "What do I have to do?"

"I don't know. We've never had a king before," Clarice giggled. "But I think you should go by your real name."

Cactus cocked his head to the side thinking about being king, then said, "Hmm. King Anthony. Has a nice ring to it... But to you, I am always Cactus."

Queen Clarice gleamed and jumped into his arms. Cactus spun his queen around and smiled. He gently released her, held her face, and said,

"Ricey... I have always been and will always be by your side. In this new world, we will make so many things possible together. You will lead our colony to greatness, and I will lead our family. We can and will have both. This is *our* new kingdom. This is *our* new life."

Queen Clarice teared up and began jumping excitedly in place as Cactus charmingly dropped down to one knee, took her by the hand, and said, "Clarice, Queen of Red Ants, will you be my wife?"

Clarice jumped into his arms again knocked him over and shrieked, "Yes!"

Suddenly, a child walked away from the huddle and was curious about a twinkling figure coming toward them.

"Look, look! Ghosts! It's a bunch of ghosts, Mommy. They are coming toward us," he shouted and pointed.

Queen Clarice and Cactus stood up to inspect this *ghost* that was coming toward them. As it got closer, this *ghost* seemed to be circular and filled with lines. The couple ran through the crowd and stood at the front to see exactly what it was. Queen Clarice gasped and yelled, "It's a web! Colony, run! Run!"

The ants scrambled and tried to pick up their scattered items while Queen Clarice and Cactus ran toward the web. The web dropped down and trapped fifty of the ants, just missing Queen Clarice. She ran over to her trapped ants while the others tried to flee. Cactus drew his sword, began cutting webs, and shouted an order to some soldiers to come and cut the web off the citizens as Queen Clarice tried to pull off the sticky strong web herself, but struggled. General Croz ran towards Clarice and yelled to the colony, "Bush spider attack! Everybody run, leave your things! Secure the seed!" He approached the queen and with calm reassurance said, "Your Majesty, take your mother's sword and protect us."

General Croz handed the sword to her, and she cut herself free from the web, sliced a hole in the sticky net freeing the captured, while the colony sprinted into the distance. Cactus ran back towards his fiancé and General Croz turned to him and mouthed 'protect my daughter'. Cactus nodded, grabbed the queen by the hand and they ran towards the colony as bush spiders ran alongside them shooting webs up into the air to trap them. Suddenly the queen broke away from Cactus and charged toward a young bush spider that chased after the children. Cactus worried for his love but continued to slice the legs of bush spiders, cut away webs, and kept checking to see what his queen was doing. As the young bush spider closed in on them, he shouted, "Gotcha now!"

Lord Kier, of the bush spiders, knocked the young spider away from the children, scowled at him then said, "This is not how we hunt. We do not hunt children!"

"Yes, Lord Kier," the young spider said and scurried away.

Queen Clarice witnessed this noble act and lowered her sword then shouted, "Lord Kier! I appreciate your mercy on our children. Please leave our colony alone."

Lord Kier slowly turned to her and said, "We just don't hunt children. The rest of you look tasty."

"Children, run!" Queen Clarice screamed.

The children scurried away, and she charged toward Lord Kier with her sword drawn. Cactus ran towards her filled with rage. She cut off one of Kier's legs and then another. He let out a shrill scream, then opened his mouth to swallow her whole. Suddenly Cactus flipped over Queen Clarice and sliced off the fangs of the beast, landed in front of his love pushed her back, and growled at the spider, "Don't touch my queen!"

As Lord Kier fell over and wriggled in pain, Cactus hoisted Queen Clarice up and tossed her on top of Lord Kier and she stabbed him in the abdomen killing him. She jumped down into Cactus' arms they smiled and each other readied their swords and ran back toward the ants. They watched in horror as some of them get swept away by webs. She stopped and shook as group after group was captured, seemingly in slow motion. *This is all my fault; I've killed us all,* she thought.

Lieutenant Cactus grabbed her hand and tried to pull her along as her sisters, and General Croz kept trying to get the citizens to run and were equally terrified. Cactus saw his love shaken by the sight and he shouted, "Queen, my queen! Ricey, run!" Queen Clarice mustered the strength to continue running towards her family and a large web fell over the top of the remaining ants and trapped them all surrounded by the tumbleweed fires that were supposed to keep them safe.

# Ten

Mala, Queen of the desert bush spiders jumped down in front of the trapping web and traced the sticky cage with the slow wicked steps of her eight legs, hissing and cackling menacingly until she approached Queen Clarice. She bent down and showed her poison-dripping fangs, then said in her serpentine voice, "So you think you can lead your colony across my land and kill my brother, the great Lord Kier, without consequence? You are mistaken, little Queen! I, am Queen Mala and you and your colony are dinner."

Queen Mala snarled, and Queen Clarice hid her fear behind a scowl as her enemy continued to pace around the web cage; Cactus grabbed for her hand, but Clarice pushed him away so that she could face her enemy alone. The evil queen paced in front of the web while her soldiers jumped around it and scared the ants. Everyone clung to each other and shook enough to make the ground beneath them tremble. Finally, Queen Clarice bravely yelled out, "Queen Mala! We are not here to stay. I was only defending my colony when I killed your brother. You have taken some of my ants, some who had families and dreams of a better future. Can we call this even?"

Queen Mala ran over to Queen Clarice with her fangs drawn and her eight eyes reflecting the fire and frightened faces surrounding them, then shouted, "You are a murderous, selfish, deceptive colony! Your mother and soldiers killed my ally, Cylon, and his soldiers. And you are trying to call this even and claim peace? No!"

Queen Mala turned away from the colony and they began the burial ceremony for Lord Kier, which included digging a hole for the dead royal and then stomping their legs aggressively around the grave to signal other spiders that a royal has fallen. Then they walk away and forget about them forever. All the soldiers started to furiously dig with all their legs creating a hole large enough to place his body in. The plan was to put the ants on top and allow any spiders to come and feast. Queen Clarice was told the sinister plans as two of the bush spider soldiers paced the web cage. They turned their backs and made their way toward the burial. The rapid thumping of the legs had begun as they shouted *Kier, Kier, Kier!* The thumps made the ground quake and Clarice shook as she awaited their fate.

Suddenly, each small fire around them was extinguished with water one by one. Queen Clarice looked up and saw Bee soldiers carrying leaves filled with water. She gasped and ordered her soldiers to stand at the ready and to keep the colony quiet. Suddenly, she felt the wind of King Larry who gently glided down and whispered, "Wait for our calls then cut your way out and run."

Queen Clarice looked back up and saw the Sphinx Moth and Bee clans flying above with the torches made from leaves and small tumbleweeds. King Larry took off and joined the rest of the soldiers as Queen Clarice whispered to Cactus, "When they give the signal, get everyone out of here. Take the seed and secure it — that is our future. Jasmine! Where is Jasmine?"

Jasmine emerged timidly from the corner and said, "Yes, Your Majesty?"

"We are going to get out of here. Make sure everyone knows that if it looks like I won't make it, they need to keep going. You will then be appointed queen and keep the royal court as is. You understand?" Queen Clarice ordered.

"Your Majesty, Sister! I can't leave you, I am not ready for this," Jasmine cried.

"Jasmine, that is an order. I must stop us from living in fear." Queen Clarice said as she petted her face to comfort her.

She watched the spiders continue to stomp and laugh evilly at their plans amongst themselves and saw that the moths were in position. Then she saw Queen Ayo emerge from her buzzing soldiers and fly in front of Queen Mala's face and said confidently, "You're never going to do better are you?"

Queen Mala sighed and rolled all eight of her eyes and said, "What are you talking about, desert pest?!"

Queen Ayo took off into the sky and screeched, "Yikikiki yikikiki!"

Then King Larry responded "Wooroo! Wooroo!"

Suddenly, the flying clans started dropping flaming leaves and tumbleweeds on the surrounding spiders. Some of the spiders curled up and died while others exploded and scattered in the desert. The red ant soldiers cut away the giant web and began running up a short hill.

Flames began to circle the battle as Queen Clarice slowly made her way through battle with her hand on her sword as pieces of flaming leaves and tumbleweed fell around her as she approached her enemy, Queen Mala.

Queen Ayo saw where Clarice was headed and screeched, "Larry! She's going for Mala! She'll be killed! We can't lose her too!

King Larry shuttered flew over to Queen Ayo then paused and said, "She must stop the evil at its source. This is no longer our fight."

A lone tear dropped from her eye, she nodded and said, "Alright, but I will clear a way for her victory." She readied two quartz blades and bellowed, "FOR RAE!"

Queen Ayo took off toward bush spider soldiers running towards their queen to protect her. She swooped down and under then over several spiders cutting their legs and abdomens. Then she took off into the sky spun around with her sword held high and shouted *Yikikikow* to signal the flying clans' soldiers to start heading back to the oasis.

Meanwhile, as Jasmine and General Croz quickly led the colony away from the battle, the colony kept looking back and yelling for their queen. Jasmine cried as she thought of her sister dying in the fire and her possible unwanted ascension to a queen. Lieutenant Cactus hurried the colony along and kept looking back for his love. He called for her and ran toward her as she made her way towards Mala. General Croz grabbed him and said, "This is her fight!"

"She is my wife!" Cactus shouted back. "Ricey! My queen, we are free. Come with me!"

General Croz grabbed Cactus' shoulders and said, "Lieutenant! She is your heart! She is my daughter! But she is our queen! And she must save us — that is her place. I know it's hard to accept. You are a soldier first and her love second. Come with me. Come with me now."

Cactus was overwhelmed with sadness and nodded to agree with the general. He stared back at his queen as she approached Queen Mala. Finally, the flames grew so big that he could no longer see her. He still stood in the distance, hoping she'd run through to him. He thought back to their adventures as children falling into the cactus leaf. How she bravely climbed into the truck. Or just that evening when he proposed to her. He took a deep sigh to hide his tears and ran back toward the colony to fulfill his duty.

Queen Clarice reached Mala and the two queens paced in a circle and stared menacingly into each other's eyes. Queen Clarice turned and bravely readied her sword. Queen Mala showed her fangs and hid her fear behind her eyes that reflected the fire and growled, "You killed the scorpions. You killed my soldiers. But you will not kill me!"

"Even if you kill me, my colony will survive… unlike yours," Queen Clarice said snidely.

Queen Mala charged, and Queen Clarice slid under her body scraped her abdomen with her sword then ran back to the front of the beast. Queen Mala let out a rage-filled scream and charged again, spitting poison, and kicking her legs. Queen Clarice avoided each kick and poisonous spit then finally chopped off one of Queen Mala's legs. She let out a shrill scream heard by every bush spider nearby. She continued to kick and spit poison at Queen Clarice when, suddenly, some poison finally struck her chest. Queen Clarice fell to the ground and quickly wiped the poison from her. She sat up and Queen Mala stood over her with her eyes still reflecting the blaze. Queen Clarice inched back, writhing in pain from the poison. Then she stood up and readied her sword and said, "No living thing will conquer me!"

She swung her sword and cut off another front leg then said, "No *beast* is too big for me!"

As Queen Mala screamed in agony, Queen Clarice stabbed her in two eyes and shouted, "I proclaim to you, desert beast!"

She grabbed onto one of Queen Mala's legs then swung her sword across the sand and set it ablaze. Queen Mala continued to groan and scream in agony as Queen Clarice swung herself on top of the wicked queen. Queen Mala gasped and turned her remaining eyes up to Queen Clarice as she raised her fiery sword above her abdomen and shouted, "I will have this victory!"

She stabbed Queen Mala in her back and the sword burned her from the inside out. Queen Clarice jumped off the evil queen's back as she screamed, rolled over then shriveled up and died next to the grave of her brother.

# Eleven

Queen Clarice rolled over and stretched out her arms in the middle of the fiery circle. The poison on her chest began to seep through her body and she became dizzy and weak. She could hear the remaining bush spiders that watched from afar stomp their legs to mourn the fallen queen. Clarice knew soon they'd be creeping up to the fire to kill her but knew the poison would take over sooner. As the fire blazed around her, she only hoped that her colony got away and that they would find the oasis. She stared up at the stars and could hear her mother's voice sing in a whispering echo. With quivering breath, she whispered back,

*You're bigger than the stars.*
*You're brighter than the sun.*
*Stand up for what you believe in*
*and your victory will be won.*
*It may cause you pain.*
*There are days you will lose.*
*But believe, sweet child,*
*nothing will conquer you.*

She took a long deep breath and the flames slowly faded from her sight, and she was in darkness.

Meanwhile, the colony watched from atop a hill and cried for their queen who sacrificed herself for them. Some of the citizens tried to run back to her but the soldiers stopped them and gave them her message. Lieutenant Cactus doubled over and screamed in agony for his fallen love, then pulled himself together to try to help the colony back in order. The saddened wails were broken by the eldest disgraced soldier's servant.

"Finally, justice is served. That wretched queen will die in the desert as she should have long ago."

Jasmine quickly turned her head and marched toward the servant and said in a stern tone, "By order of our beloved queen, I am to be appointed queen in the event of her death. Our sister has sacrificed herself so we can move on and prosper. So, my first order as queen is to banish this worthless and disgusting waste of space from our colony."

"How dare you, you have no power!" the servant yelled.

Jasmine leaned forward and said, "Over you I do. Guards, when we leave make sure she stays behind and does not enter our new home."

The soldiers pushed the servant away as the colony scowled at her and shook their heads. The second servant glared at the elder ant servant she once idolized and said, "I am disgraced because of you, I have always been. It's time for me to make my own choices now. Goodbye, disgraced *one*."

The elder servant quivered as her once faithful follower faded away from her sight with her haunting dismissal. She screamed and cried while she thought about her fate alone in the desert. Jasmine turned around and continued to watch as the remaining bush spiders slowly surrounded Queen Clarice. Suddenly, whipping and snapping sounds surrounded the fire, followed by shrill screams from the spiders. Jasmine looked closer and tried to see what the noise was through the flames and the colony jumped around to get a view of the commotion. Suddenly, a child yelled out, "Scorpions! They are headed for the queen!"

"She will not suffer them again! General, ready the soldiers!" Jasmine ordered.

With fury in their hearts General Croz and Cactus drew their swords and lined up the soldiers to attack, she looked closely and saw that the scorpions were fighting and killing the spiders. Then she saw that they stood around the fire to protect Queen Clarice. The bush spiders scurried off and Jasmine lifted her hand and said, "Stand down. They are protecting our queen."

While the spiders continued to run, a group of scorpions walked up to the colony. Everyone inched back and the rest of the soldiers rushed up to the front, armed and ready to fight. Jasmine was curious about their actions, as they approached, she defensively asked, "What are you doing here?"

"Please don't be alarmed. I'm not here to attack the colony," the scorpion said.

Jasmine nodded and motioned for the soldiers to lower their weapons. Aid Dora snapped, "What are you going to do? Help us then ambush us when we reach our new home?"

"The last ambush never should have happened. We were misled by Cylon. As a scorpion nation, we have nothing against you. So, after his death, we decided to watch over you to repay the debt of lives lost that night. You are Lady Seven, right?" the scorpion asked.

"Y-yes. It's Jasmine now." Jasmine quivered.

"Don't you remember me from that night when I looked inside the colony? I'm Samer... King Samer. I shamefully served as Cylon's lieutenant. I knew about the ambush and started to tell you when I saw you. After the war, I vanished to start my colony with the ones who were strong enough to go against Cylon's beliefs and his followers. I'm here now as a new King and one day my son will take my place. We will continue to watch over you. Can you forgive us for following a poor leader?" King Samer said.

Happy tears dropped from Jasmine's eyes and then nodded. King Samer insisted that they collect the queen and keep moving while the scorpions keep the bush spiders away. Jasmine explained the queen's wishes and he hesitantly agreed. The lieutenants of the bee and sphinx moth soldiers shared the route to the oasis and took off. The remaining colonies slowly backed away from the raging fire and continued their journey. Cactus was the last to leave as he tried to wait and see if his love survived. As the flames slightly parted and he saw his queen still laying lifelessly on the ground, took a somber breath, wiped a tear from his eye, whispered *'By your side, always.'* and then followed behind the colony.

# Twelve

Sunrise in a crystal-like sky was revealed to Queen Clarice's slowly opening eyes. She took a deep relieving sigh then popped up and realized she was riding on King Larry's back with a small bee sitting by her side holding a small piece of an aloe plant. The bee explained that she is a healer and removed the poison that Mala spat on Clarice's body. The queen turned around to look ahead and saw her colony was nearly at the oasis and smiled. Then she gasped and jumped when she saw the scorpions surrounding the colony.

"King Larry! The scorpions will kill them; we have come too far! Please stop them, oh sun and moon please!" Queen Clarice begged.

"Shhhh. Not to worry, Your Majesty. They helped you keep from getting eaten as you slept and have promised to protect them under King Samer's orders," King Larry said.

Queen Clarice stuttered in a panic, "W-Who? Never mind. But why? They killed us, they attacked us!"

"Cylon forced many of his clan to do that. King Samer and his followers wanted nothing to do with it. Now rest, Your Majesty. We'll catch you up later. We are almost there, and you have a colony to start," King Larry said, calmly.

She laid back down with her arms stretched wide and flew on King Larry's back and happily felt the calming wind on her face. As they approached the oasis, the healing bee took off to join the celebration as the queen listened to the families and her court cheering joyously and hugging each other shouting *'We did it!' 'It's real!' 'We're going to live!'* The children ran toward the blooming and colorful oasis while some of the scorpions happily jogged alongside them. Queen Clarice sat up on King Larry's back and held on as he dove toward the oasis and swooped around the land so the queen could see her happy colony.

The flying clans swooped through the oasis in celebration while the children played in the running stream. The flying clans showered bright flower petals and shouted, *'Yikikikow!'* Queen Ayo swooped around the new colony and then led her clan in singing *"You are welcome here, you are loved here, you are a part of this colony. Come on you are welcome, come on you are welcome, come on you are welcome! This is home!"* The sphinx moth clan began blowing horns made of tree bark and the bees jumped to the ground with some running to drums made from woven grass and paddle plant leaves and others encouraging the ants to dance. Meanwhile, the soldiers carried the watermelon seed into the tall grass and began to dig and plant the seed.

Cactus and the court stood at the grassy river shore and smiled as they gazed at the happy colony. Then they all sunk their heads while they remembered their loss; Cactus began to cry and crouched down to the ground rubbing his face in distress as he mumbled, "We made it Ricey. We'll make you proud."

King Larry swooped around the oasis once more and whistled to get everyone's attention as he made his landing in the tall grass behind the planted watermelon seed. He walked out from the grass and looked confusedly at the colony who stopped mid-dance and said, "Well, aren't you going to bow?"

"For you, King Larry?" General Croz asked jollily.

King Larry grinned and said, "For your queen."

Everyone cocked their heads to the side in confusion, then Queen Clarice gracefully stepped out from the grass. She smiled and chuckled a bit as she panned the crowd of dropped jaws and shocked looks. The crowd remained in stunned silence while she continued to walk forward. Finally, the silence was broken when she asked with a big grin, "So how was your trip?

Jasmine ran through the crowd and screamed, "Sister!"

She ran into Queen Clarice's arms followed by the colony cheering and running to surround their queen. She hugged and kissed most of her citizens and the royal court. Lieutenant Cactus ripped off his armor and sword and ran toward his beloved. He swooped her up and kissed her and said playfully, "Don't scare me like that, Ricey!"

\*\*\*

The morning was spent in celebration of her return and gobbling up every type of food that was available on the oasis. Queen Clarice sat and told the story of her victory to the hundreds of children that clapped and cheered for her bravery. Cactus looked on with pride and held the hand of his queen.

As Clarice was shown the land by Queen Ayo, King Larry sat with Cactus who asked how Clarice survived. King Larry explained that after everyone headed to the oasis he thought back to when the first ambush happened, and Queen Rae was left behind. Seeing Clarice laying in the circle fire made him think of all the heartbreak Queen Rae felt when she was left and mistook it for a test of strength and made everyone suffer for the sake of tradition. Then he said,

"I feared that Clarice would survive, and no one would be there for her the way she had been there for them. That type of loneliness breeds hatred. So, I went back with the healer bee, collected her, and here we are."

"But she told us to move on though. I didn't want to, she commanded us to," Cactus stated

King Larry smirked and said, "Yes, I know. She won her battle and so she deserved her joy. As her elder, it was important for me to create a path for her to create her joy."

Cactus smiled and the two kings continued to sit and express their joy.

The next morning, the official coronation of the queen began. She stood on top of a rock as General Croz placed her new crown on her head. The crown was woven with swirls and arches and a red jewel in the middle and some draping on her face to stand for the prosperity growing from the watermelon seed. Her council and sisters dressed her in a new royal scarf that was woven together from all her sisters' scarves. The collective colonies gathered around her. Queen Clarice stood by a very proud Cactus, looked out at her colony, and smiled then the queen lifted her hands and bellowed,

"My ants, thank you for trusting me enough to keep going. We're here! Bee, Scorpion, and Sphinx Moth clans, thank you for your loyalty and protection. We are proud to live among you once again! I, along with my fellow leaders, am open to suggestions about how we will live here because this home is for all of us. We are now privileged with such an abundance of life and food. I will not deny that I am saddened by the losses that we suffered of some of our family, friends, and soldiers. But I know that they are in the stars and watching us as we celebrate this new life. If you want your dream to become real, you must do the terrifying act of facing what defends you the most, your doubt. Once you face it, there is no limit to the possibilities that grow from the simple act of taking a chance. I wish that we did not have to battle for so long and endure such grief. It was not a perfect journey, but we made it! We are a strong unified nation! We will thrive!"

The crowd jumped joyously! The Bee clan shouted *yikikikow*! The Sphinx Moths bellowed *wooroo wooroo*! The Scorpion clan yelled *mikimiki*! The Red Ant colony cheered, and Jasmine led a bird-like song '*Here we are! Here we are! Here we are!*' for their incredible queen.

\*\*\*

For the next four crescents, the elder royals and their young royals, Queen Clarice, and Lieutenant Cactus made plans to expand the colony and make sure everyone lived bountiful lives. Although Cactus was anxious to marry his queen, he knew that a strong foundation for their colony was more important.

Each spring they celebrated the watermelon harvest where hundreds grew and fed thousands. They did not grieve long over the sorrows that got them to their land. To comfort anyone who missed their loved ones, they'd gather at the river to stare at the stars and when the stars began to twinkle, they knew their loved ones were looking back at them and the colony danced in the light that reflected on the water.

In every moment they had in the oasis they rejoiced and lived in harmony with the other clans. They remembered their history and accepted the past, but always moved forward. Some married, some worked, some had families of all types, and some had it all. They were happy and healthy and that is all that mattered to the royals.

Just after Clarice's $22^{nd}$ crescent, at sunset, Anthony and Clarice stood in front of the colony and said their vows. Both wore long capes woven from silk for the ceremony. Anthony wore blue to represent the peace of the new nation and Clarice wore red to represent the passion to live a fruitful life. Since there had never been a wedding the couple was unsure what to say. So they held each other's hands and said, *'No matter the battle or the joy I am by your side.'*

General Croz clapped and encouraged the new colony to cheer and said, "Colony, I present to you, Queen Clarice, and our first King Anthony!"

Clarice and Anthony had three girls and three boys who all eventually had five children each of their own. Upon Clarice's thirty-eighth crescent, she gladly passed on her crown to their eldest daughter, Amelia. Clarice enjoyed the rest of her life in the colony, with her husband, children, and grandants.

\*\*\*

There is a Red Ant colony that lives amongst the Bee, Sphinx Moth, and Scorpion clans in the most productive and humid oasis in the desert. They were led there by a dream of a watermelon seed that saved and fed thousands for generations because a young queen believed in the possibility of prosperity.

Lightning Source UK Ltd.
Milton Keynes UK
UKHW020648050722
405403UK00010B/886